Scruffy Teddy
and the lost ball

p

Scruffy Teddy is playing ball. Whoops!

Where did the ball go?
Behind the gate?

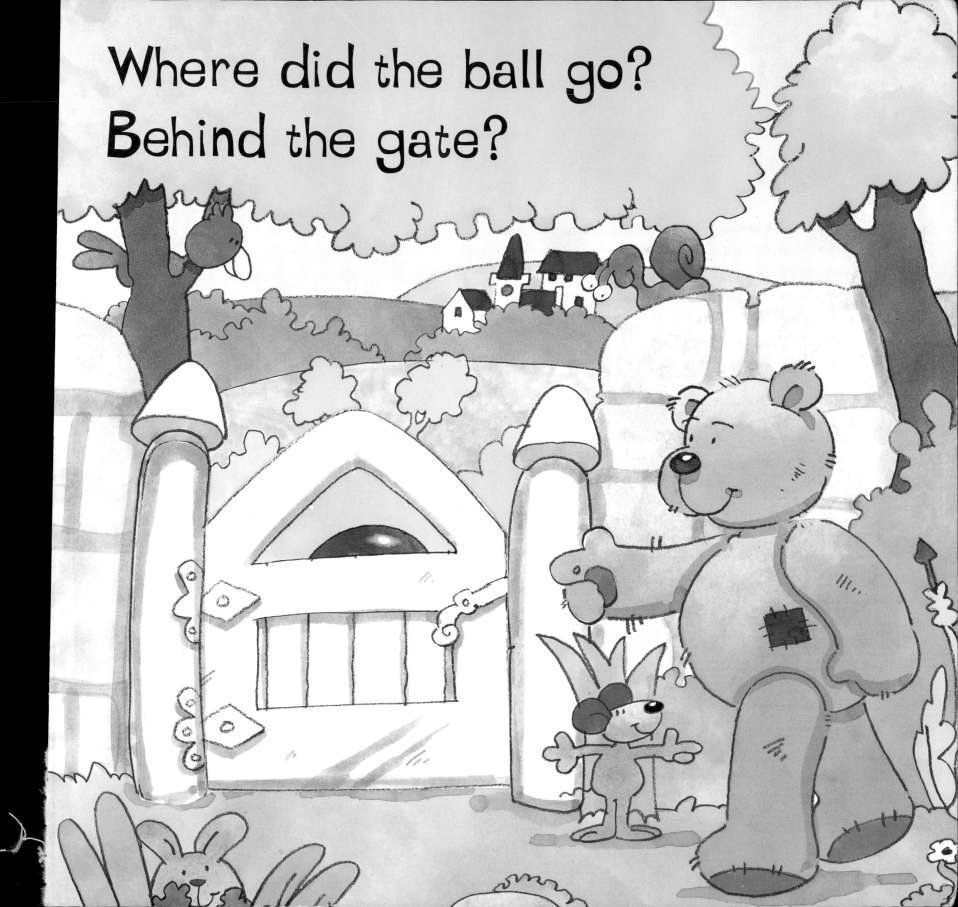

Look, there it is, in the pond!

Well, that must be it on the chair.

Did it bounce into that car?

Could that be it behind the hedge then?

Has Scruffy found it at last?

Should he look behind the watering can?

Does that look like
the ball?

Well, that must be it, surely?

Could that be the ball
in the branches?

Or in the pond?

Scruffy's out of luck, he'll have to go back home.

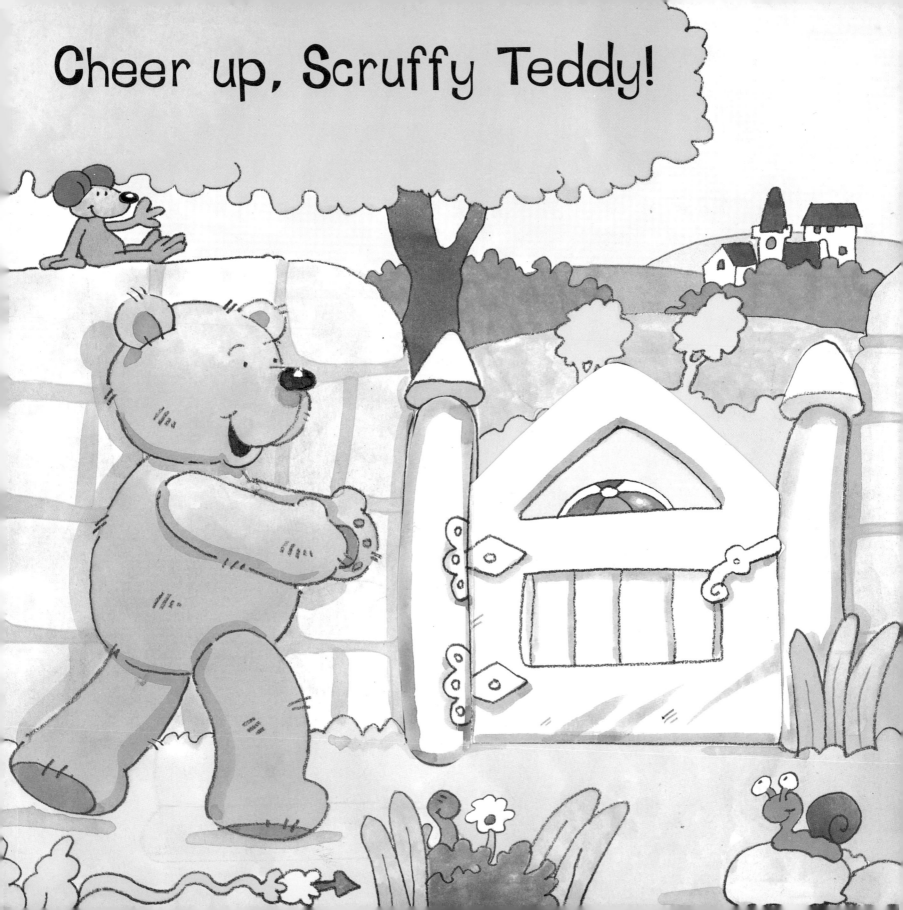

Cheer up, Scruffy Teddy!

Look out for lots of other exciting books
with your favourite bear-
Scruffy Teddy!